SADIE

AND HER NEW WHEELS

BY LINDA ZIMMERMAN

www.OrisonPublishers.com

To Sadie, thank you for inspiring me to tell your story.
A story of friendship, courage, and acceptance.
You will always have a special place in my heart.

My name is Sadie. I am a big, friendly dog.

I love to play Frisbee with my best buddy, Matt, and my dog sister, Annie.

I love to run up and down the field when Matt plays soccer. I would be an awesome goalie.

I love to play with the neighborhood dogs—and even with Gracie, a spunky neighborhood cat.

I especially love chasing squirrels.

But one day, one of my back legs felt strange. It felt like it was asleep, and it would not wake up.

Mom and Dad took me to Dr. Liz. She said I have a condition that will cause both back legs to become weak, making it hard to walk.

She gave me special food and yucky-tasting medicine. When it's time to take my medicine, I hide and cover my mouth. Do you hide and cover your mouth too?

Dr. Liz said that walking on a treadmill in water and swimming would make my legs stronger. As long as I don't eat too many hot dogs at the snack bar!

But I missed playing with my friends. It made me sad to lie outside when others were playing, even though Gracie brought her favorite toy mouse for me to bat around.

**Mom and Dad and Matt were sad too.
Even the squirrels were sad!**

Gracie said everyone loved me, and I was a lucky dog, even though my legs were weak. But I did not feel lucky. That night, I prayed to be a good role model for other dogs like me with special needs.

Then Mom had an idea. She took me to meet Theo and Bailey, who have weak legs just like mine. But they have special wheels to help them walk and play.

"It takes work to learn to use wheels," Mom said.

"Would you like to try?"

"Would I? You bet!" I told her.

I chose pink wheels because I love the color pink. Every day my friends and I stared out the window, waiting for my wheels to arrive.

Finally, the delivery truck pulled up. I howled with joy!

I watched patiently as Dad opened the big box and got busy putting my wheels together. Mom bought me a pink collar, a pink leash, and pink boots to match my wheels.

Finally, my wheels were ready. I was excited but also a little scared. I took one small step, then another. All of a sudden, I was walking. I went faster and faster, and then I was running!

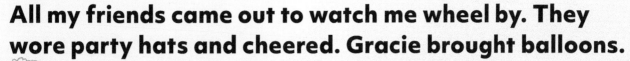

All my friends came out to watch me wheel by. They wore party hats and cheered. Gracie brought balloons.

Now I can play Frisbee and soccer again.

I can play with my friends. I can chase squirrels.

There is nowhere I can't go and nothing I can't do.

Yes, my legs are weak, and I will always need my wheels. But I am not much different from my friends. Not really.

Aren't we each a little different on the outside? Some tails are stubby, and some are long. Some noses are short, and others are pointy. Some ears are small, and some are large.

Some of us are big and fast, and some are tiny and not so speedy.

We are different colors, and some are many colors.

And some need a little help. Just like me.

Do you know anyone who could use a little help?

MY WHEELS OF WISDOM

Love one another.

Accept that it is okay to be different.

Remember that friendship is better than biscuits.

Always give squirrels a head start.

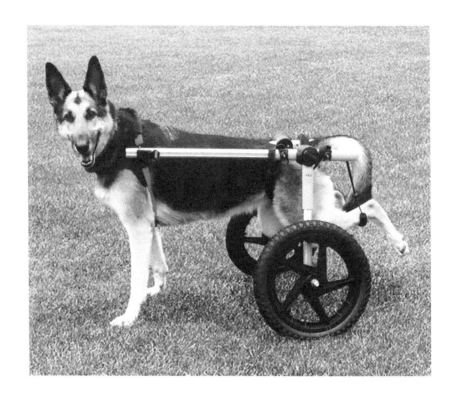

Meet Sadie, the inspiration for *Sadie and her New Wheels*. A friendly, and playful German Shepherd whose life changed suddenly when at the age of 8, she was diagnosed with Degenerative Myelopathy (DM). DM is a progressive disease that affects the spinal cord resulting in paralysis of the hind legs. There is no cure or proven treatment that can stop the progression of DM.

As Sadie's legs became weaker, she received a set of wheels. With her new wheels she was back playing, running and enjoying her daily walks. It was amazing the number of children and adults who wanted to know more about this dog in wheels. It was on these walks that the author realized that Sadie had a story to share.

To learn more about Sadie's wheels, please log onto www.WalkinPets.com.

CPSIA information can be obtained
at www.ICGtesting.com
Printed in the USA
BVHW021101301121
622865BV00022B/1152